P9-BZD-268

Rita
the Frog Princess Fairy

Special thanks to Tracey West

If you purchased this book without a cover, you should be aware that this book is stolen property. It was reported as "unsold and destroyed" to the publisher, and neither the author nor the publisher has received any payment for this "stripped book."

Text copyright © 2016 by Rainbow Magic Limited

All rights reserved. Published by Scholastic Inc., *Publishers since 1920*. SCHOLASTIC and associated logos are trademarks and/or registered trademarks of Scholastic Inc. RAINBOW MAGIC is a trademark of Rainbow Magic Limited. Reg. U.S. Patent & Trademark Office and other countries. HIT and the HIT logo are trademarks of HIT Entertainment Limited.

The publisher does not have any control over and does not assume any responsibility for author or third-party websites or their content.

No part of this publication may be reproduced, stored in a retrieval system, or transmitted in any form or by any means, electronic, mechanical, photocopying, recording, or otherwise, without written permission of the publisher. For information regarding permission, write to Scholastic Inc., Attention: Permissions Department, 557 Broadway, New York, NY 10012.

This book is a work of fiction. Names, characters, places, and incidents are either the product of the author's imagination or are used fictitiously, and any resemblance to actual persons, living or dead, business establishments, events, or locales is entirely coincidental.

ISBN 978-0-545-85197-8

10 9 8 7 6 5 4 3 2   16 17 18 19 20

Printed in the U.S.A.   40

First edition, January 2016

Rita
the Frog Princess Fairy

by Daisy Meadows

SCHOLASTIC INC.

The Fairyland Palace

Fairy Tale Lane

Rachel's Hou

Tippington Town

The Fairy Tale Fairies are in for a shock!
Cinderella won't run at the strike of the clock.
No one can stop me—I've plotted and planned,
And I'll be the fairest one in all of the land.

It will take someone handsome and witty and clever
To stop storybook endings forever and ever.
But to see fairies suffer great trouble and strife,
Will make me live happily all of my life!

Contents

Story Time

"There are so many fairy tales in the world," Rachel Walker said. "Do you think we'll ever read them all?"

"I'm going to try!" promised her best friend, Kirsty Tate. "And I'm excited to hear a new one today!"

The girls were walking to the garden at Tiptop Castle. They were there for the

Fairy Tale Festival. Every day, the organizers had fun fairy tale themed activities for the guests to do.

Both Rachel and Kirsty loved fairy tales—and fairies, too! They had first met each other—and real fairies—on Rainspell Island. They had been best friends ever since.

"Look, there's the storyteller!" said Kirsty, pointing.

A woman in a long, pale-yellow dress stood in the middle of the garden. She had dark, curly hair with a white flower in it and a frog puppet on her hand. Rose bushes in bloom with tiny pink blossoms surrounded her. Colorful butterflies danced on the flowers.

Rachel sighed happily. "This whole place is so magical!"

The girls sat in white chairs set up in the garden for Fairy Tale Time. The other kids there for the festival looked just as excited as they were to hear the storyteller.

"I just thought of something," Rachel whispered into Kirsty's ear. "Jack Frost stole the magic objects from the seven Fairy Tale Fairies. He wants to be the star of every fairy tale. Does that mean that he'll be in the storyteller's fairy tale?"

"I didn't think of that," said Kirsty. "We'll see, I guess." She shrugged.

Jack Frost was always trying to cause trouble for the Fairyland fairies. A few days ago, he had taken the Fairy Tale Fairies' magic objects. Until the objects were returned to the fairies, the characters in those fairy tales wouldn't be in the right stories. The girls had helped the Fairy Tale Fairies find three magic objects so far. But four more were still missing.

The storyteller spoke up. "Welcome, everyone! Gather round. I am Sarah the

Storyteller. Today I will tell you the story of *The Frog Princess*, a Russian fairy tale."

"I've never heard that one before," Kirsty whispered to Rachel.

The children in the garden quieted down as the storyteller began.

"Once upon a time, there were three princes, each looking for a wife. 'Each of you will shoot an arrow, and where it

lands, you shall find your wife,' ordered the king."

"That is a strange way to find a wife," Rachel remarked in a whisper.

"The first two princes shot their arrows, which landed by beautiful maidens," Sarah continued. "But the third prince's arrow landed by a frog. The king didn't care. Rules were rules. So the third prince married the frog and she moved into the castle with him."

"Then the king ordered a test to see which bride was the best," said Sarah. "Each princess had to bake him a cake. 'How can a frog bake a cake?' the prince wondered. But he did not know her secret."

"What secret?" a boy in the crowd asked.

"The frog was really a princess under a spell," Sarah explained. "Her name was Vassilisa. When night fell, Vassilisa transformed from a frog back into a princess. She called on her attendants to help her. And then . . ."

Sarah frowned. "And then, um, there were some green goblins. I think. But I'm not sure." She shook her head. "I'm sorry, everyone. I can't seem to

remember the
story. Can we
try again
later?"

The
children got
up and left
the garden,
disappointed. Poor Sarah
looked very confused.

Rachel pulled Kirsty aside. "Oh no! I
bet Jack Frost is around here somewhere,
trying to take over The Frog Princess
fairy tale!"

"We have to stop him!" Kirsty said.

Too Many Frogs

Rachel looked thoughtful. "If Jack Frost is taking over the fairy tale, then maybe Vassilisa, the Frog Princess, is here, too."

Kirsty nodded and looked up at the sun. "It's daytime, so she would be in her frog form. So we need to look for frogs!"

"Frogs like water," said Rachel. "And Tiptop Pond isn't far from here. Let's go!"

The girls ran across the castle grounds until they came to Tiptop Pond. The pond's blue water sparkled in the afternoon sunlight. Green lily pads floated on the pond's surface.

"This is the perfect place for frogs," said Kirsty. "I'm sure we'll find her."

The girls
shaded their
eyes from
the sun and
looked
across the
water.

"What's that?
On that lily pad
over there?" Rachel asked.

"It looks like a frog!" Kirsty said
excitedly, and they walked around the
pond to get closer.

They stood on the shore and peered out
at the frog.

"Is that frog wearing clothes?" Kirsty
asked.

Rachel nodded. "A jacket with tails,
and a shirt with a ruffled collar. But

that's not something a princess would
wear!"

"That's because I'm not a princess!"
the frog said. He hopped onto the shore.
Then he stood on two legs and bowed.
"Bertram the Frog
Footman, at your
service."

"Bertram! Of
course! It's nice to see
you again!" said
Rachel. She and
Kirsty had met
Bertram many times
before in Fairyland.

"The King and Queen of Fairyland sent
me here to help find Vassilisa the Frog
Princess," Bertram said. "As you can see, I
am especially qualified for the job."

Suddenly, a
sparkling light filled
the air.

Poof! Rita the
Frog Princess Fairy
appeared.

"Yes, you are
perfect for this fairy
tale, Bertram!" she said.
"Who better to help find a Frog Princess
than a Frog Footman?"

Kirsty and Rachel had met Rita when
they visited Fairy Tale Lane. She had
long, wavy hair and wore a green dress
with puffed sleeves.

"Hi, Rita!" said Rachel.

"Rachel and Kirsty, you two were very
smart to come looking for the Frog
Princess at the pond," she told them.

"I have been looking everywhere for her. Can you help me find her?"

"Of course!" the girls both said at once.

"There are lots of places around the castle where frogs might go," said Rachel. "Like the moat."

"Or the fountain," Kirsty suggested.

Bertram hopped between them. "If you don't mind, I think I have an idea," he said.

"We don't mind at all," said Kirsty, smiling at the frog.

Bertram cleared his throat. Then he made a very loud sound.

"*Ribbit! Ribbit!*"

The sound echoed all over the castle grounds. Seconds later, replies came from echoing back.

"*Ribbit! Ribbit!*"

Rachel's eyes widened. "Look!" she cried. "There are frogs everywhere!"

Every frog at Tiptop Castle had heard Bertram's call. They hopped across green lawns and stone walkways toward the pond.

"There are a lot of frogs!" said Kirsty. "How will we know which one is the princess?"

"I can help with that," said Rita, fluttering her wings.

As the frogs got closer, Rita flew over them, waving her wand. Glittering, tiny green frogs and stars sprang from it.

"Where are you, Vassilisa?" Rita asked, waving her wand again.

The shimmering frogs and stars floated through the air and landed on one of the frogs.

"Over here!" Rita cried.

Kirsty and Rachel made their way over to the glittering frog, careful not to step on any other frogs. Kirsty picked her up. She looked a little bit different than a normal frog. Her green skin was very smooth, and her eyes were a pretty shade of blue.

Rita happily clapped her hands. "We did it! We found the Frog Princess!"

Jack Frog?

Rachel got a closer look at the frog in
Kirsty's hand.

"She's a very pretty frog," said Rachel.

"And a very lovely princess," added
Rita, flying above the Frog Princess.
"But unless I can get her back into her
fairy tale, the story will no longer be

about her. It will be about that horrible Jack Frost!"

Rachel looked around. "He must be around here somewhere. What magic object of yours did he take?"

"My silver mixing bowl," Rita replied. "With it, I can bake the tastiest treats!"

"I can't imagine Jack Frost making anything tasty," said Kirsty.

"We must find that rascal, then," said Bertram.

"What should we do with Princess Vassilisa?" Kirsty asked, looking down at her hand.

"We can bring her to our room," suggested Rachel. "She'll be safe there."

"Good idea," said Rita. "You girls do that, and Bertram and I will start looking for Jack Frost."

"We won't be long," Rachel promised, and the girls raced back to the castle. They crossed the bridge that passed over the moat. They went through the beautiful grand entryway of the castle and climbed up the stairs to the top of one of the castle's tall towers.

Rachel pushed open the door to their room. It contained two four-poster beds draped with pretty canopies. Kirsty set the Frog Princess on top of the polished wood dresser.

"That doesn't look very comfortable," Rachel remarked.

Kirsty took a pillow from her bed and placed it on the dresser. The frog hopped on it.

"That's better," said Kirsty. "But maybe she needs some water."

"And she might be hungry," said Rachel. "Let's go to the kitchen."

Kirsty waved to the Frog Princess as

they left the room. "We'll be right back!" she promised.

The girls ran down the stairs to the kitchen. A cook in a white jacket greeted them with a friendly smile.

"May I help you?" she asked.

"Yes, please," said Rachel. "May we have a snack?"

The cook looked thoughtful. "Well, it's awfully close to dinner . . ."

"It's for a friend of ours . . . who missed lunch," Kirsty said. It wasn't really a lie. She just didn't mention that her friend was a frog!

"In that case, there's some fruit in

the refrigerator," she said. "Help
yourself."

"Thank you!" the girls said, and they
opened the refrigerator.

"What kind of food do frogs eat?"
Kirsty whispered.

"Bugs, mostly," Rachel said. "But she
is a Frog Princess, so I'm sure fruit will
be fine. Let's get grapes. Everybody loves
grapes."

They put some grapes in a small bowl
and went back up to their room. Rachel
put the grapes next to the frog and Kirsty
filled the bowl with water from the
bathroom sink. The Frog Princess
happily ate one of the grapes. Then she
drank some of the water.

"I think we're all set," said Rachel.
"Let's go find Jack Frost!"

The girls went back outside. They were
on their way back to Tiptop Pond when
they saw a frog hopping toward them.
But this wasn't an ordinary frog. It was
a very big, very ugly frog!

"*Ribbit! Ribbit!*" the frog said. "I am a
frog, but tonight I will turn into a
princess."

Rachel and Kirsty exchanged a confused look. That voice sounded very familiar . . .

"That's no frog. That's Jack Frost dressed in a frog costume!" Rachel whispered.

Kirsty took a step toward the strange-looking frog. "We know it's you, Jack Frost." Kirsty bravely called out. "Give us Rita's magic mixing bowl!"

"Never!" he said and he began to hop faster, away from Rachel and Kirsty. "Goblins! Deal with these pesky girls!"

Four goblins, who were also wearing frog costumes, came out of the bushes and hopped toward Rachel and Kirsty.

"Where are Rita and Bertram?" Rachel wondered.

"I don't know," said Kirsty. "But we have to get that mixing bowl. Come on!"

She and Rachel chased after Jack Frost. But his legs were much longer than theirs and he could hop surprisingly fast. The four goblin frogs ran between Jack Frost and the girls. One of them stuck his big frog foot in front of Kirsty. The other stuck his foot in front of Rachel.

Whomp! The girls tripped and fell onto the grass. They could hear the goblins giggling as they hopped away.

"Oh, dear! Are you all right?"

Rita appeared in a cloud of
shimmering fairy dust, looking worried.

Kirsty and Rachel stood up, brushing
grass off themselves.

"I'm okay," Rachel replied. "What
about you, Kirsty?"

"I'm fine," Kirsty said, "except that
Jack Frost has gotten away!"

"That's all right," said Rita. "If I know

him, he won't go far. I'm just glad that you two are okay."

"Where is Bertram?" Rachel asked.

"I don't know," Rita answered. "We split up to find Jack Frost and I haven't seen him since."

Then one of the fairy tale organizers stepped out onto the bridge. All of the organizers dressed like fairy tale characters for the festival, and he was dressed like Puss-in-Boots.

Rita quickly flew behind Rachel so she wouldn't be seen.

"Dinner, everyone!" the festival organizer called.

"We need to go in," Rachel said.

Rita nodded. "Don't worry. I'll stay close by."

The girls headed inside the castle and ate in the big dining room with the rest of the kids attending the festival. They kept an eye out for Jack Frost, but didn't see anything unusual.

After a yummy meal of Snow White's Spaghetti with Friendly Giant Meatballs, they went back outside to look for Jack Frost. The sun was setting, and the sky was growing dark.

"We should get back to our room and check on the princess," Rachel said.

The girls headed back up to their room high in the tower. As they walked down the hall, Rachel noticed a weird glow coming from under the door.

"Rita? Is that you?" she whispered, pushing open the door.

But it wasn't Rita. Bright light filled the room. When it faded, a woman stood in front of them. She wore a long, green dress and a golden tiara that glittered on her dark hair.

Rachel glanced at the dresser. The frog wasn't there. That's when she realized what had happened.

"The frog has turned back into a princess!" she cried.

Trouble in the Kitchen

The Frog Princess looked around, confused.

"My room seems different than usual," she said.

"That's because it's *our* room," Rachel explained. "It's kind of a long story. You see—"

"I don't have time for a long story. I

have to bake a cake before the sun comes
up!" the princess said, and she rushed
past the girls and out of the room.

"We've got to help her!" Kirsty cried,
and the two girls ran after the princess.
Suddenly, two goblins jumped in front
of them.

"Stop right there! We're under orders to
keep you from messing up Jack Frost's
fairy tale," they said.

"It's not his fairy
tale!" said Kirsty.
"He stole it!"

Poof! Just then,
Rita the Frog
Princess Fairy
appeared in front of
them. She waved her
wand at the two goblins.

"You two
are not being
very nice,"
she said. She
waved her
wand again and
tiny frogs hopped through the air toward
the goblins. There was a shimmer of
fairy magic and they were transformed
into two very startled-looking frogs!

Rita turned to Rachel and Kirsty. "We
need to hurry. They won't stay like this
for long. Let me turn you into fairies,"
she said, and she waved her wand again.

The sound of tiny bells filled the air as
the fairy dust worked its magic on the
girls. They shrunk down to fairy size and
could feel fairy wings sprout on their
backs.

"I love being a fairy," Rachel whispered.

Kirsty nodded in agreement as she turned to follow Rita.

"The princess should be in the kitchen, so we'll look for her there," Rita said.

They flew past the frog goblins, down the stairs, and into the kitchen. The cooks had cleaned all the counters and it was shut down for the night. Rita motioned for the girls to be quiet. The Frog Princess was nowhere in sight— but Jack Frost was!

Jack Frost was no longer wearing his frog costume from the afternoon. Instead, he wore a gold tiara on his head and stood in front of a stainless steel worktable. The table was a mess of

baking supplies: flour, sugar, eggs,
measuring cups, spoons, and bowls.

Rita, Rachel, and Kirsty flew behind
some cans of food on a shelf so they could
watch Jack Frost without being seen.

"Time to bake a cake!" he said. Then
he called out, "Royal attendants, come
here and bake me a cake!"

"Who is he talking to?" Rachel asked.

"It's from the fairy tale," Rita explained. "Vassilisa says it after she transforms from a frog into a princess. Her attendants help her bake the cake."

But no royal attendants came into the kitchen. Instead, four goblins came in, shoving and pushing each other.

"Bake me a cake!" Jack Frost barked.

"But we don't know how to bake a cake," one goblin whined.

"Then figure it out!" said Jack Frost. "In the fairy tale, the Frog Princess bakes the best cake ever. I need to do the same thing!"

Grumbling, the goblins started grabbing the items on the table. One goblin cracked an egg into a bowl, shells and all!

"Not like that!" said another goblin. He grabbed a second egg from the carton, but he squeezed it too hard! The yolk dripped down his arm and onto the floor.

The third goblin dumped a bunch of flour into the bowl without even measuring it. The fourth goblin picked up the bag of sugar—and the bottom fell out. The sugar spilled all over the floor!

"No, no, no. You're doing it all wrong!" Jack Frost said angrily.

"Do we need more eggs?" asked the first goblin, smashing more eggs into the bowl.

"NO!" Jack Frost yelled. Then he snapped his fingers. "Wait! I forgot the most important thing!"

Then he reached under the table and pulled out a beautiful silver bowl.

Rita gasped. "My magic mixing bowl!"

Jack Frost placed the bowl on the table.

"With this bowl, we can bake the best cake ever!"

"We've got to stop him!" Kirsty said.

Rachel nodded. "We need a plan."

Suddenly, Vassilisa ran into the kitchen.

"I finally found the kitchen! Now excuse me, please," she said, pushing past Jack Frost. "I need to use this table. I have to bake a very important cake."

She picked up the silver mixing bowl.

Jack Frost grabbed it out of her hands. "Oh, no you don't! This is my fairy tale now! I am baking this cake! Goblins, remove her!"

The four goblins grabbed Vassilisa by the arms.

"Your hands are sticky!" the Frog Princess complained as the goblins pulled her away from the kitchen.

"Oh, dear!" said Rita. "I must go help her. You girls stay here and get that mixing bowl back, if you can!"

"We will!" Kirsty promised.

Achoo!

Rachel and Kirsty watched Jack Frost from their hiding place.

He rubbed his hands together. "Who needs those lazy goblins? I can make the best cake ever, all by myself!"

Jack Frost picked up a measuring cup and dipped it into the bag of flour. A

little cloud puffed out
of the bag and hit
Jack Frost's nose.

"Achoo!" Jack
Frost sneezed.

Rachel's eyes lit
up. "I think I have a
plan!" she said. Then
she whispered in Kirsty's ear.

Kirsty nodded. "That should work."
The two girls slowly flew out from
behind the food cans. Jack Frost was
frowning, holding the empty egg carton.

"I need more eggs!" he grumbled, and
then he picked up the mixing bowl
and walked to the refrigerator.

"Now!" Rachel said.

The girls flew as fast as they could to
the bag of flour. They dove inside and

each came up with two big handfuls of flour. Then they flew out of the bag.

"You two!" Jack Frost cried, spotting them.

Rachel and Kirsty each took a deep breath. Then they blew on the handfuls of flour as hard as they could.

Whoosh! The flour flew at Jack Frost, hitting him right in the nose!

Jack Frost's nose twitched. And twitched again. And then . . .

"*ACHOO!*"

He let loose with a big sneeze, bigger than before. It sent Rachel and Kirsty tumbling backward across the air. It also caused Jack Frost to drop the silver mixing bowl! The magic bowl clattered onto the floor.

"I've got it!"

Rita flew back into the kitchen and touched the mixing bowl on the floor. It shrunk down to fairy size in her hands.

"*Noooooo!*" Jack Frost wailed. He shook his fist at Rita. "Give that back right now!" He lunged at the fairy.

Rachel and Kirsty felt a
little dizzy after being
tumbled around by the
sneeze. But they
righted themselves and
flew to help Rita.

Just then, Bertram the
Frog Footman hopped
into the kitchen, followed
by Princess Vassilisa.

"I just wanted to bake a fairy tale
cake," Jack Frost pouted. He stomped his
foot and disappeared in a cloud of
freezing-cold ice magic.

"Bertram showed up as the goblins
were taking the princess away," Rita
explained to the girls. "He helped me get
her back."

Bertram gave a little bow. "I told them I knew frog-jitsu," he said, winking.

"You were marvelous," Princess Vassilisa said with a lovely smile.

"Thank you for saving my mixing bowl, girls," Rita told them. "Now I need to take it back to Fairyland so Princess Vassilisa can return to her fairy tale."

"And I must return to the king and queen," said Bertram.

Rachel looked around the messy kitchen. Flour and sugar covered the floor, egg yolks dripped from the table, and Jack Frost's dirty dishes were stacked high.

"I guess Kirsty and I
need to get this
cleaned up," Rachel
said, and then she
yawned. It had been
a long day.

Rita smiled. "Don't
worry," she said. "I've
got this."

Rita waved her wand, and fairy magic
glittered in the air. In an instant, the
messy kitchen was sparkling clean!

"Amazing!" said Kirsty.

"And now we really must go," said
Rita. "Thank you again, Rachel and
Kirsty!" She waved her wand, returning
Rachel and Kirsty to human size.

Rita twirled her wand again and she,
Bertram, and Vassilisa began to

shimmer. In seconds, they had disappeared in a whirl of fairy dust, leaving Rachel and Kirsty alone in the kitchen.

Rachel yawned again. "I'm so glad we helped save The Frog Princess fairy tale. But I am so tired!"

"Well, I'm hungry," said Kirsty. "All I can think about now is cake!"

Laughing, the girls headed back up to their room.

Tea-Party Time

"You know what the next best thing to cake is?" Kirsty asked the next morning at breakfast.

"What?" asked Rachel.

Kirsty grinned. "Pancakes!" she said, happily taking another bite of one of the fluffy pancakes on her plate.

Rachel laughed. "I think you're right!"

The guests at the Fairy Tale Festival ate breakfast at the long banquet table in the castle's dining room. Just about everyone was wondering what the fairy tale event of the day would be.

Then a festival organizer walked into the dining room. He was dressed as the Big Bad Wolf. Two cooks followed behind him.

"Good morning, everyone," he said. "I hope you are enjoying your Peter Pancakes."

"We are!" the guests all cheered.

"I'm here to announce a special event for this afternoon," he said.

"This morning we came into the kitchen to see that our cooks had made some beautiful mini cupcakes. So this afternoon we'll have a fairy tale tea party!"

Everyone clapped and cheered. Rachel noticed that the cooks looked confused and were whispering to each other. They walked past the girls.

"I didn't make those cupcakes," said one.

"Neither did I," said the other.

"Then who did?" asked the first one.

The second cook shrugged. "Maybe some magical fairies came into the kitchen last night and made them? I wouldn't be surprised. It seems that a lot of strange things have happened since this fairy tale festival began."

Rachel and Kirsty looked at each other and smiled. They both knew who had made those cupcakes. "Rita!"

That afternoon, the girls headed back to the garden for the fairy tale tea party. Scattered among the rose bushes were small round tables topped with lace tablecloths. On each table was a teapot, four teacups, and four plates. And on each plate were two of the prettiest

miniature cupcakes the girls had
ever seen!

Rachel and Kirsty took a seat at one of
the tables. Rachel picked up one of the
cupcakes. It had pale-green frosting with
tiny green frog sprinkles on the top! The
second cupcake on her plate had white
frosting and glittering silver star-shaped
sprinkles.

"I think they're all different," Kirsty said. "Look, this one is pink with tiny pink heart sprinkles, and this one is purple with a yellow sugar flower in the center."

"They're all so pretty!" Rachel said. "Only a fairy could have made these."

Then Sarah the Storyteller walked into the garden, holding her frog puppet.

"Good afternoon, everyone," she said. "I'm sorry for what happened yesterday. I'd like to make it up to you today by finishing the story of *The Frog Princess*. There aren't any goblins in it at all. In fact, I don't know where on earth I got that idea!"

"But we do," Rachel whispered to Kirsty.

"And now that Rita has her magic mixing bowl back, The Frog Princess fairy tale is back to normal," Kirsty said.

"Let's make sure," Rachel said, as she took a book from her pocket. The words on the cover sparkled: *The Fairies' Book of Fairy Tales*. The fairies had given it to them in Fairyland.

Kirsty leaned in as Rachel flipped through the pages. The first three tales told the stories of *Sleeping Beauty*, *Snow White*, and *Cinderella*. They had helped rescue all of those fairy tales from Jack Frost.

Rachel turned the page to the fourth story in the book.

"The Frog Princess," she read out loud. "It's here!"

Kirsty flipped through the rest of the book, and saw only blank pages.

"Three more fairy tales to go," she said. "Which Fairy Tale Fairy do you think we'll help next?"

"I don't know," said Rachel. "But I'm excited to find out!"

RAINBOW magic™

THE FAIRY TALE FAIRIES

Rachel and Kirsty found Julia's, Eleanor's,
Faith's, and Rita's missing magic objects.
Now it's time for them to help

Gwen
the Beauty and the Beast Fairy!

Join their next adventure in this
special sneak peek . . .

Fairy Tale Creatures

"When I get back home, I'm going to try to make some of this fairy tale food," Kirsty Tate said. "These Peter Pancakes are delicious!"

"And so is this Fairyland Fruit Salad," agreed her friend, Rachel Walker.

The two girls were in the big dining room at Tiptop Castle. The tables were filled with boys and girls who had come for the Fairy Tale Festival. Each day, the festival organizers had fun activities planned for them.

Just being in the castle was like living inside a fairy tale. The meals were served on pretty silver plates, and all the food had a fairy tale theme. The Peter Pancakes were shaped like fairy wings. The Fairyland Fruit Salad came in a crystal goblet with a tall stem.

Kirsty sighed. "I wish this festival never had to end," she said, taking another bite of pancake.

A hush came over the room as Amy, one of the organizers, stood up. She was dressed as a princess in a pink dress with a pointy pink hat on top of her blond curls.

"Good morning, fairy tale fans!" she began. "We have a very exciting event planned tonight. It's the Creature Costume Party!"

The kids all began to whisper excitedly.

"There are many marvelous creatures in fairy tales," Amy said. "Unicorns, dragons, talking bears—the possibilities are endless. We have set up the ballroom with all the supplies you will need to make your costumes for tonight. So have fun, and use your imaginations. There will be prizes for the best costumes!"

Kirsty turned to Rachel. "It's fun that we get to make our own costumes!"

Rachel nodded. "I know. What do you think we should be?"

"I don't know." Kirsty frowned. "A unicorn would be fun."

"I bet a lot of people are going to be unicorns," said Rachel, looking thoughtful. "To win a prize, we should be something really different. Like a . . . a griffin!"

"What's a griffin?" asked Kirsty.

"It's a half-lion, half-eagle," Rachel said.

"A griffin sounds interesting," Kirsty agreed. "Or maybe we could be some kind of sea serpent!"

"We should look at the fairy tale books in the reading room," Rachel suggested. "I'm sure we'll find some good ideas there."

"That sounds like a great plan," Kirsty said.

Then Rachel looked around the dining room. She lowered her voice so only

Kirsty could hear her. "Besides making our costumes for the party tonight, we also need to keep an eye out for the Fairy Tale Fairies."

"And for mean Jack Frost," Kirsty added.

Kirsty and Rachel were friends with the fairies in Fairyland. On their first day at Tiptop Castle, Hannah the Happily Ever After Fairy had come to see them. She took them to Fairy Tale Lane in Fairyland.

There they learned that Jack Frost was causing trouble again. He had stolen the magic object belonging to each of the Fairy Tale Fairies! Jack Frost wanted the fairy tales to be all about him.

Now the fairy tale characters were missing from their stories. Kirsty and

Rachel had helped the Fairy Tale Fairies find four magic objects so far. But they still had three more objects to find—and three fairy tales to save.

"So far, every character we've met has been somewhere in the castle," Rachel said.

"Or on the grounds," Kirsty added. "The Frog Princess was hopping across the lawn."

"And Jack Frost was nearby every time!" Rachel said.

The girls finished breakfast and left the dining room. They walked through the grand entrance hall. A glittering chandelier shimmered over their heads. In front of them, two suits of armor stood guard in front of a wide staircase.

Rachel was about to open the door to the reading room when Kirsty nudged her.

"Rachel, look!"

A tall man came down the staircase. He wore a fancy blue velvet suit and a shirt with a ruffled collar. But his hands and face were covered in brown fur! He had pointy ears, a black nose, and tusks, too.

"That must be one of the fairy tale organizers," Rachel guessed. "He's dressed like Beast from *Beauty and the Beast.*"

Then they heard the sound of tinkling bells. The doorknob Rachel had just been holding shimmered with fairy magic. When the magic settled, a tiny fairy was perched there.

"That *is* the Beast!" she cried.

"Quick! In here!" Kirsty whispered.

The fairy followed the girls as they ducked into the reading room. The Fairy Tale Festival was full of amazing sights. But Kirsty and Rachel would have a hard time explaining to everyone that they knew a real fairy!

RAINBOW magic™

Which Magical Fairies Have You Met?

- ❑ The Rainbow Fairies
- ❑ The Weather Fairies
- ❑ The Jewel Fairies
- ❑ The Pet Fairies
- ❑ The Dance Fairies
- ❑ The Music Fairies
- ❑ The Sports Fairies
- ❑ The Party Fairies
- ❑ The Ocean Fairies
- ❑ The Night Fairies
- ❑ The Magical Animal Fairies
- ❑ The Princess Fairies
- ❑ The Superstar Fairies
- ❑ The Fashion Fairies
- ❑ The Sugar & Spice Fairies
- ❑ The Earth Fairies
- ❑ The Magical Crafts Fairies
- ❑ The Baby Animal Rescue Fairies
- ❑ The Fairy Tale Fairies

■SCHOLASTIC

Find all of your favorite fairy friends at
scholastic.com/rainbowmagic

HiT entertainment

ASTIC and associated
are trademarks and/or
ered trademarks of Scholastic Inc.
Rainbow Magic Limited.
d the HIT Entertainment logo are
marks of HIT Entertainment Limited.

RMFAIRY13

RAINBOW magic™

Magical fun for everyone!
Learn fairy secrets, send
friendship notes, and more!

SCHOLASTIC and associated
logos are trademarks and/or
registered trademarks of Scholastic Inc.
© 2015 Rainbow Magic Limited.
HIT and the HIT Entertainment logo
are trademarks of HIT Entertainment
Limited.

■ SCHOLASTIC

HiT entertainmen

www.scholastic.com/rainbowmagic

RMACTIV

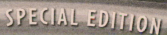

RAINBOW magic™

SPECIAL EDITION

Which Magical Fairies Have You Met?

- ❑ Joy the Summer Vacation Fairy
- ❑ Holly the Christmas Fairy
- ❑ Kylie the Carnival Fairy
- ❑ Stella the Star Fairy
- ❑ Shannon the Ocean Fairy
- ❑ Trixie the Halloween Fairy
- ❑ Gabriella the Snow Kingdom Fairy
- ❑ Juliet the Valentine Fairy
- ❑ Mia the Bridesmaid Fairy
- ❑ Flora the Dress-Up Fairy
- ❑ Paige the Christmas Play Fairy
- ❑ Emma the Easter Fairy
- ❑ Cara the Camp Fairy
- ❑ Destiny the Rock Star Fairy
- ❑ Belle the Birthday Fairy

- ❑ Olympia the Games Fairy
- ❑ Selena the Sleepover Fairy
- ❑ Cheryl the Christmas Tree Fairy
- ❑ Florence the Friendship Fairy
- ❑ Lindsay the Luck Fairy
- ❑ Brianna the Tooth Fairy
- ❑ Autumn the Falling Leaves Fairy
- ❑ Keira the Movie Star Fairy
- ❑ Addison the April Fool's Day Fairy
- ❑ Bailey the Babysitter Fairy
- ❑ Natalie the Christmas Stocking Fairy
- ❑ Lila and Myla the Twins Fairies
- ❑ Chelsea the Congratulations Fairy
- ❑ Carly the School Fairy
- ❑ Angelica the Angel Fairy
- ❑ Blossom the Flower Girl Fairy

3 stories in each one!

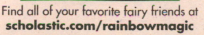

SCHOLASTIC

Find all of your favorite fairy friends at
scholastic.com/rainbowmagic

SCHOLASTIC and associated logos are trademarks
and/or registered trademarks of Scholastic Inc.
© 2015 Rainbow Magic Limited.
and the HIT Entertainment logo are
trademarks of HIT Entertainment Limited.

HIT entertainment

RMSPECIAL17